This Little Tiger book belongs to:

Sophie

Anne

Kathryn

Farley   FKKS aBB

For Poppy, with love ~ M C B

For Toby ~ F E

LITTLE TIGER PRESS
1 The Coda Centre, 189 Munster Road, London SW6 6AW
www.littletiger.co.uk

First published in Great Britain 2008
This edition published 2014
by Little Tiger Press, London

Printed in China • LTP/1900/0825/0114

10 9 8 7 6 5 4 3 2 1

The Wishing Star

M. Christina Butler

Frank Endersby

LITTLE TIGER PRESS

Little Brown Mouse and Little Silver Mouse were best friends. They did everything together.

"I'm so glad you come with me on my adventures," said Little Brown Mouse. "It wouldn't be much fun by myself."

"I am so lucky to have you as a friend," said Little Silver Mouse. "I couldn't climb this high without you!"

They went everywhere
together and always
took care of
each other.

They shared everything, even
their biggest secrets and
special dreams.

One night, as the two friends sat
planning their next adventure, they
saw a glittering star shoot across
the sky and fall into the lake.

"It's a Wishing Star!" cried Little
Brown Mouse. "We can make a wish
if we find it!"

He raced down the hill. "Come on!"
he shouted. "We'll go down the river
in our boat!"

"All the way to the lake?" Little
Silver Mouse squeaked, running after
him. "That's dangerous!"

But by the time he caught up, Little Brown Mouse was pushing their boat into the water.

"Hurry!" he called. "We need to find the star before anyone else does!"

As they floated down the river, strange shadows moved through the reeds in the moonlight.

"Are you sure we're safe?" Little Silver Mouse asked nervously.

Little Brown Mouse didn't answer. He was paddling with all his might and thinking about what he would wish for when they found the star.

"I could wish to have an exciting adventure every day!" he said, paddling harder than ever.

"And I could wish for a magic pantry that is always full of nuts and berries," began Little Silver Mouse dreamily.

"No! No!" shouted Little Brown Mouse, leaping up. "We can only have one wish, because there is only one star!"

"But we need food for the winter!" cried Little Silver Mouse, stamping his foot.

"I saw the star first!" Little Brown Mouse replied crossly. "The wish belongs to me!"

And as the two mice argued, the boat rocked and twisted around and around, until . . .

all at once, it bumped into the
reeds and stopped. The mice
peered out into the darkness.
"Is this where the water
monsters live?" whispered
Little Silver Mouse, trembling.

He grabbed onto Little Brown Mouse.
There was something rustling in the reeds!
    "Eeeek!" he squeaked with a jump, as two
bright eyes stared out at them.
    "What are you two doing here?"
cried Vole in surprise.

Little Brown
Mouse sighed with relief.

"Please help us, Vole. We're
on our way to find a Wishing Star
that's fallen in the lake, but now
we're stuck!"

"A Wishing Star?" Vole shivered
with excitement. "I could wish for
a fresh bed of grass every day, and
then I won't have to make my bed
anymore!"

"Did you say a Wishing Star in the lake?" croaked Frog, hopping up out of the river. "I could wish for as many flies as I can eat!" And with a huge leap, he was gone!

"Quick! Let's go!" cried Vole, jumping into
the water and giving the mice new paddles.
"We can't let Frog get there before us!"
    Vole pushed the leaf boat from the reeds,
then scrambled aboard as the wind took hold
of it and sent them speeding down the river.

Twirling and swirling, the boat
was swept back and forth between
the rocks. Little Silver Mouse held
on tightly and thought about his nice,
warm bed under the oak tree, when
suddenly he heard a loud CROAK!

"Look over there!" he cried out. "Frog's trapped on the rocks! We need to help him!"

"I suppose so," muttered Little Brown Mouse, guiding the boat across to Frog. "Even though he was going to take *our* wish!"

"Thank you," Frog spluttered as Little Silver Mouse pulled him to safety.

They huddled together as the boat
swirled on, until at last the water grew
calmer and slower as they came nearer
to the lake.

"One more bend," said Vole eagerly,
"and we'll be there!"

Gently they drifted onto the lake, and there before them were hundreds of shimmering Wishing Stars!

"*Look!*" gasped Little Silver Mouse. "We can *all* have a wish!"

"And you can go first," said Little Brown Mouse.

Little Silver Mouse smiled and thought hard.

"I wish," he said slowly, "I wish . . . that I'll always have good friends like you!"

And they all agreed—that was the best wish ever!